DUCK FOR COVER & OTHER TALES

A COLLECTION OF SHORT STORIES

BARBARA VENKATARAMAN

CONTENTS

A DISH BEST SERVED COLD

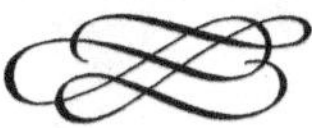

Howard tracked the horrible smell to the farthest corner of his yard. It was a dead skunk, the only thing that smelled worse than a live one. He was sure Mack had tossed it over the fence to piss him off and his first instinct was to toss the carcass back, but he decided against it. *Good fences don't always make good neighbors*, he thought, *but they do keep me from punching mine in the face.* Their longstanding feud had been simmering for a while and now it was about to boil over. Retaliation was Howard's specialty and he relished it.

"Jake!" he hollered to his son. "Get your lazy self out here. Bring a shovel."

The boy didn't dare keep his father waiting and soon appeared dragging a shovel that was too heavy for him. He looked younger than his ten years with his slender build, pale complexion, and scrawny legs scraped in a recent bike accident. When he saw the putrid skunk he cringed, enraging his father.

"You're too damn soft, Jake! All you do is play video games—it's your mother's fault. That's why you live with me now."

Struggling to hoist the shovel the boy muttered "I'd rather live with my Mom." What he thought was *I hate you.*

Howard laughed which did nothing to improve his cruel features. "Your mother didn't fight hard enough for you, kid, and her lawyer was a hack, so suck it up. Don't give me attitude or you'll regret it."

He returned to the house leaving Jake to his odious task. Sipping a cold beer, his first of the morning, Howard made a list of the many ways he could burn Mack, anonymously, of course. His cell rang but when he saw it was his ex-wife he turned it off. Maria needed to learn who was boss. Hint: it wasn't her. He knew she had telephone privileges with Jake but he could always say he hadn't heard it. What could she do about it? Absolutely nothing. She left him one of her cryptic voicemails: *Love your enemies, do good to those who hate you.* His ex-wife was a religious nut and he blamed that wacko church group she hung out with. Who goes to Bible Study five times a week?

An hour later, Jake came back in, filthy and exhausted. "Did my mom call?"

"Nope," Howard lied. "Take a shower, son, you reek."

After his third beer Howard's plan to exact revenge on his neighbor had taken shape. There were several stages, each one an escalation of the one before. Starting with the fun stuff, he applied for a credit card in Mack's name and went on a buying spree. He ordered every magazine and newspaper he could think of, set up appointments with home improvement companies to come to his neighbor's house, and asked the Jehovah's Witnesses to pay Mack a visit. He called phone sex lines and charged it to the card after ensuring the bills would go to Mack's house for his wife to see.

The following week, Howard heard his neighbors arguing loudly through his open window and laughed with delight. He walked out into his yard to better enjoy the show but immediately started gagging. This time, there were a dozen rotting skunks scattered all over. Howard was so furious he thought he might stroke out. He didn't bother to call Jake. Instead, he grabbed the shovel and hurled every last one of them over the fence as hard as he could. Several of them landed in Mack's pool with a satisfying splash. That night, Howard dressed in black and sneaked over to Mack's house where he proceeded to flatten the tires on both cars. For good measure, he siphoned all the gas too.

The next morning, the police knocked on his

door to ask him about the skunks and the damage to the cars. He made up an alibi, dragged Jake out of bed to gain sympathy, and they eventually went away. At noon, Mack showed up and banged on the front door screaming obscenities but Howard ignored him. Cowering in a corner, Jake asked if he could call his mother. Howard ignored him too.

It was time to jump to phase two of his plan. Howard went online and set up dozens of fake email addresses before going on Yelp to leave scathing reviews of Mack's hardware store. Howard was so consumed with his scheme that he called in sick to work that week and barely paid attention to Jake, who was living off peanut butter sandwiches and playing video games non-stop. Mack had stopped leaving angry messages on Howard's voicemail and had hired a lawyer to send threatening letters demanding he cease his harassment. As Howard was throwing the lawyer's unopened letters in the trash he saw candy wrappers.

Quaking with rage, he confronted Jake. "Where did you get the candy?"

Defiant, the boy said he bought it. Howard slapped him in the face.

"Don't lie to me! Where did you get it?" he demanded.

In a quavering voice, Jake replied "Mom gave it to me. I rode my bike to the park and she was there."

With a newfound calmness his father said. "You're grounded. No more bike rides for you."

Jake stormed off to his room but didn't dare slam the door.

The next day, child services called to ask why Jake wasn't in school but Howard let it go to voice-mail. In the afternoon, Maria showed up at his door but he pretended not to be home. After she had gone he found a note taped to the front door that said: *The meek shall inherit the earth.* He tore it up.

Crazed with alcohol and irrational revenge fantasies Howard was totally consumed with taking down his perceived enemy. That afternoon, he rented a bulldozer to knock down Mack's house while he was at work even though he had never operated heavy machinery in his life. By the time the bulldozer was delivered Howard was drunk and paid scant attention to the instructions or the strong warnings about the dangers. He gleefully hopped onto the bulldozer and started it up. After mashing the gears in every direction Howard was jerked forward and fell off his perch into the street where he was promptly crushed. Hoisted with his own petard, as Shakespeare would say.

That evening, Jake's mother showed up with a social worker to pick up her son. After a joyful reunion they packed up his things and started the drive home.

In the car, Maria turned to her beloved child and

gave him a gentle smile. "Jake, you know that God helps those who help themselves, right?"

Jake looked at his mother, bewildered. "Sure, I guess so."

"What I'm trying to say is I'm very sorry about the skunk."

THE YES MAN

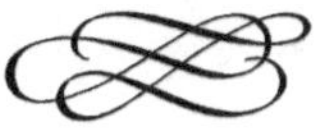

Unopened boxes are stacked on every chair; magazines blanket the dining room table. Athletes, celebrities, and fashion icons on glossy covers watch as I shove their magazines onto the floor. After giving them a solid kick for good measure I rip open one of the boxes to find last year's collection of Southern Cooking recipes.

"What the hell, Dad?" I show him the cookbook.

He just smiles and shrugs. Of course he does. Senility has embraced him like a happy drunk, erasing his crabbiness and impatience and somehow transferring them to me. I dig through the piles of mail until I find confirmation that my dad has indeed subscribed to enough magazines to open a newsstand and enough cookbooks to audition for Food Network. Cookbooks are as useful to my dad as a subscription to Teen Vogue or Western Horseman, which he now also has. In my fifty years I'd never seen him cook anything except a scrambled egg and now he couldn't even do that because his range was shut off. The assisted living facility blamed the insurance company's fear of fire, and their aversion to writing big fat checks. My internal monologue is interrupted by a text from my friend Lena.

We're grabbing dinner at the new Mexican place, you in?

Sounds fun but I'm taking care of my dad's latest misadventure. Next time, promise.

Taking a deep breath, I call the magazine/cookbook subscription center. I plan to be courteous but things go downhill fast.

"I need to cancel all of these subscriptions," I say, "and you need to remove every single charge."

"May I ask why?"

"I'll tell you why. You took advantage of an elderly man with obvious dementia. You should be ashamed of yourself. I'm ashamed for you. How do you sleep at night? There's a special place in hell—"

"No problem," he says. "I cancelled them. As a family member, you can also participate in these special offers—"

"—Are you seriously trying to sell me something right now?"

"This offer is good until midnight—"

"Stop talking! I have to ask you something before I hang up."

"Yes?"

"Did my father subscribe to anything else?"

"Yes, he did."

I sigh. "What?"

"Chocolate of the month."

"He's diabetic. Cancel it."

"Cheese of the month."

"He has high cholesterol, cancel."

"Vacation club."

"Are you kidding? He's on permanent vacation, cancel."

"Cigar of the month."

"He has COPD, cancel it." I don't know why I feel the need to go down this rabbit hole, but I do. "What else?"

"The shopping club."

"I will contest every charge. Cancel it. Is there more?"

"Online dance lessons."

I laugh at the absurdity. "Cancel."

"Beer of the month."

"Not allowed to drink. Cancel. Wine club too?"

"Yes."

"Cancel. What else?"

"Book of the month, Golden Oldies CD Club, shot glasses from around the world, Franklin Mint coin club—"

"Cancel everything."

"I need you to put that in writing."

"I need to know your name so I can sue you."

Pause. "I canceled everything."

"Good, send confirmation in writing today."

"Is there anything else?"

"Don't call my dad again or I'll file a class action on behalf of every octogenarian in America."

"You have a nice day."

As soon as I disconnect, a call comes in. My neighbor Carmen invites me to join her walking club to get some exercise. I say I'll think about it.

I escort my dad down to the lobby and he shows me around the facility, our ritual. Bingo room, dining hall, movie theater, nursing station. Everywhere we go people seem genuinely glad to see him. The old ladies flirt with him and he flirts back. They don't mind that he can't remember their names. He's a Canasta Casanova, a dowager's Don Juan. Fortunately, he still knows my name and remembers who I am even though we have the same conversations over and over. It's always Groundhog Day in my dad's world.

We sit down and drink coffee, our other ritual. He beams at me. "I'm so happy to be here."

"That's great, Dad. Do you know where we are?"

He looks around, thinks about it for a minute. "I'm home," he says.

I study his face. "Tell me, what's the secret to being happy?" I'm genuinely curious.

My dad reaches over and holds my hand. "The secret to being happy is...whenever someone asks you to do something, just say yes."

LIVING MY BEST LIFE

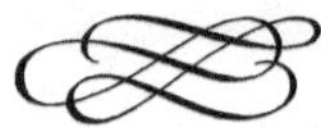

KEITH FELT LIKE HE WAS HAVING AN OUT-OF-body experience. Seated in the last row of the small theater, he was also on stage, the lead singer of a tribute band. He knew all the riffs, all the moves—because they were his. Keith's fingers ached to play guitar again, to sing the lyrics he'd written fifty years before, but those days were gone. It was surreal to watch this man channel his essence, his younger self, a pop star with three hit songs and a platinum record. That was the before time, the best time. Being inducted into the Rock and Roll Hall of Fame had always been his dream but, when it finally happened, he was an old man and Brad, their drummer, hadn't lived to see it. Three divorces and all that time on the road, had it been worth it? He hated touring; crowds weren't his thing. What he loved was creating new music and breaking all the rules, those days when anything was possible.

Keith looked around expecting to see middle-aged fans brimming with nostalgia, but there were young people too. Time was he couldn't go anywhere without being mobbed, he even had to hire security at one point, but now he was invisible. The irony of going unrecognized here, of all places, by his most ardent fans made him laugh. It was like being a ghost at your own funeral.

Listening to the music began to overwhelm him even though he'd written these songs and performed them thousands of times. Hearing *Joey* transported him to the birth of his son and the rush of love he'd felt. *Silver Heart* colored his mind with memories of Brad and their long friendship. The audience was singing along, smiling, laughing, enjoying themselves. Just two hours before, Keith had resented this man imitating him, performing his songs, soaking up the glory and living Keith's best life, but now he felt nothing but gratitude. His music would live on, his legacy, and this tribute band was a bridge to his old fans and his new ones. Who could've imagined he would get new fans at this point in life? This was the greatest gift, better than being in the Rock and Roll Hall of Fame. Keith rejoiced, reveling in his new perspective. Suddenly, the crowd started cheering. The lead singer pointed and the spotlight turned toward the audience who finally saw him sitting among them. They began chanting "Keith! Keith! Keith!" as the frontman enthusiastically motioned him over. Without hesitation, Keith joined the band on stage for one last gig.

THICKER THAN BLOOD

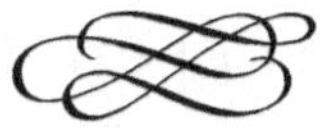

"Are you crazy, Kathy? Do you want to ruin our lives? That's what you're saying." Ben was so furious he couldn't even look at his sister.

She raised her voice. "That's not true! I just need to know, we all do. Tell him, Mark."

Without a word, Mark picked up his guitar from its stand by the sofa and softly strummed, the same way he had dealt with his parents' vicious arguments as a teen. The youngest of the three, he had borne the brunt of it after his siblings moved away.

Ben walked to the window and surveyed the dingy warehouses below. The gray skies and threatening clouds reflected his state of mind. He took a calming breath, his wife's favorite piece of advice. It helped a little. Without turning around, he posed a question, keeping his tone neutral.

"Why do we need to know, Kathy? Tell me your reasons."

She nodded. "Fair question. I feel like not knowing is as bad as knowing. I mean, if we never learn the truth we'll assume the worst. It's like Schrodinger's cat, if you don't open the box to see if the cat is alive, it's both dead and alive at the same time. Does that make sense?"

Ben turned to her, maintaining his calm, miraculously. "So, your reason is morbid curiosity? What about the consequences? You're not married, you don't have a reputation in the community, but what about me? My family will suffer, my kids will be ostracized. I could lose my job."

Mark said something so quietly they weren't sure he had spoken. Kathy walked over and laid her hand lightly on his shoulder. "What did you say, Mark? We want you to weigh in. It's your life too."

He rested his guitar on his knees. "The rumors are already swirling around and they'll never stop, so we may as well learn the truth. The damage is done. And what about the families? Don't they deserve closure?"

Ben's face paled as he tried to control his anger. "Is their peace of mind worth sacrificing ours?"

Nobody answered. Ben knew either one of them could take action on their own; this was only a group decision because they had agreed to it. This was the family reunion from hell, misery loving company.

"Think about my children," Ben said. "How will they ever date, or marry? I'm begging you to let this be. As for the families, I grieve for them—but we can't bring their loved ones back. They're gone and it's not our fault. Our consciences are clear. We shouldn't have to pay for crimes we didn't commit."

"Sins of the Father." Mark's voice sounded almost robotic, devoid of emotion.

A silence fell as each one tried to solve this unsolvable puzzle.

"Are you sure we weren't adopted?" Kathy's laughter broke the tension. "Maybe Mom was unfaithful?"

"Three times?" Ben shook his head. "Not likely."

"You're right, I guess." Kathy was blasé, like this wasn't the biggest decision of their lives. "If we did agree to do this, who would pay for our psychotherapy? That's not cheap, you know."

Ben sighed. When the FBI had approached them they had experienced all the stages of grief. Kathy seemed stuck in denial while he was firmly planted in anger. And his brother, where was he? Hard to say. Mark felt everything so deeply. When his childhood friend Leigh Ann had died, he barely spoke for a year. If Ben felt guilty about anything it was about not being there for Mark.

Kathy poured herself a glass of Pinot from the bottle in Mark's fridge. "We're so unlucky," she said, after downing half the glass. "This craze to trace your family roots, didn't it seem harmless? Just fun and games. Sure, some people learned some family secrets or found relatives they didn't know about but it wasn't supposed to solve murders--"

"--Or destroy innocent people," Ben finished her thought.

"Think about it. Just a swab of the mouth opens Pandora's Box." Kathy polished off her glass of wine. "Ben, do you believe in nature, or nurture? Are we doomed because of our DNA?" Tears began to flow down her cheeks. "Are we evil?" she whispered.

Ben's face softened; he walked over to his sister and comforted her. "We're not evil. You're not evil. If he committed those heinous crimes, those unspeakable acts, he was a monster. Anyone tracing their family tree will find a monster if they go back far enough."

"But not their father," Mark said bitterly.

Kathy was sobbing as Ben held her close. "We have to tell the FBI we won't do it," Ben said. "It would break us."

Mark stood up. "It's too late. I sent in my swab already."

Kathy gasped. "Why, Mark?"

A peaceful look settled on his face and his eyes were clear with purpose. "I did it for Leigh Ann. Her family has a right to know."

THE DEVIL'S WORKSHOP

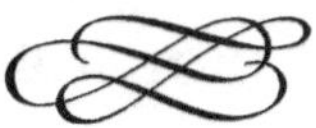

THE PROBATION OFFICER APPRAISED THE GANGLY teen slouching in the chair across from him. The boy's bored expression and lousy attitude were de rigueur for first-time juvvy offenders, like they all watched the same TikTok video or something.

"You could be in jail right now," the officer said matter-of-factly.

"Whatever, man. Just tell me what I gotta do," the teenager replied, defiant.

The officer laughed. They all think they're so badass. "You ever hear of *Scared Straight*, Noel?" The boy shook his head. "'Course you haven't. It was a program in the 70's where juvvy offenders visited lifers in prison who screamed in their faces about the horrors of prison. It was brutal."

Noel flinched. "Did it work?"

The officer turned back to his computer. "Not even a little. Lucky for you. Now, your program is more like summer camp." He chuckled to himself. "Community service and restitution. Like they say, idle hands are the Devil's workshop."

"I gotta pick up trash or something?"

The man finished typing and sent the paperwork to the printer next to his desk.

"There's more to it, my friend. Tell him what he's won, Johnny!" The officer swiveled in his chair and switched to an announcer voice. "This fine contestant has won three months' probation. With passing grades and good work reports he'll win the Grand Prize!"

"What's the Grand Prize?" Noel asked, interest piqued.

"You get to stay out of jail. Sign here."

It was Monday after school and Noel was standing inside a large warehouse filled with broken cars. There were tools and machinery everywhere but no people. *Born To Be Wild* was blasting from a speaker somewhere.

"Hey! Anyone here?" he shouted. After riding two buses he'd be pissed if he was in the wrong place.

The music cut off and a muffled voice replied "Hold your horses, will ya? Give me a dang minute."

As Noel searched for the source, a man with bushy white hair slid out from under a red Ford Mustang. He was lying on a wheeled plastic board, holding a flashlight. It hadn't occurred to the teen to look for people hiding under cars.

"You better have a good reason for interrupting my favorite song." The man wiped his oily hands on a rag as he gave Noel an appraising look. "If you're selling something, I ain't interested."

The boy scowled. "This is bullshit, man! They told me to come here--"

The man laughed. "Right! You're the new kid. I'd know that attitude anywhere—I got one just like it. Want a Coke?"

Noel relaxed. "Sure."

"Help yourself, fridge is over there." He pointed to the back wall. "Grab me one too."

Noel came back with two cans and the man chugged his down. After wiping his mouth with his sleeve he belched loudly.

"Better out than in, I always say." He grinned, exposing crooked teeth. "Here's the deal, new kid, you be here on time three days a week, I don't care which ones. Do what you're told and we'll get along fine. Got it?"

Noel shrugged. "Like I have a choice."

With a laugh the man said "You always have a choice. Door number one or door number two. Pick the wrong one and it slams shut behind you." He tossed the soda can in the trash. "You can call me Roy, by the way. Ready to work?" Without waiting for a response he said "Pour sawdust on all the oil spills you see, sweep it up and throw it away. Don't skimp on the sawdust and whatever you do, don't slip in the oil. I got no insurance." He turned his pants pockets inside out. "What you see is what you get."

Noel picked up the bag. "Am I getting paid for this?"

Roy nodded. "Course you are. Ten bucks an hour."

"For real?"

"Yeah, but you won't see any of it, it's going to your restitution. That's the breaks, kid. Do the crime, do the time."

Roy returned to the Mustang and rolled back under. The music started up again and Noel was introduced to *Werewolves of London*. From under the Mustang he could hear Roy say "Now, this is my favorite song."

Over the weeks, Noel did everything he was told: sort tools and put them away, clean headlights, vacuum cars, replace wiper blades, change bulbs, check tire pressure, and refill wiper fluid. Each time, Roy would show him what to do just once and expect him to get it right. He always did. Noel worked steadily but found himself distracted watching Roy take cars apart and reassemble them like a 3-D jigsaw puzzle with strange pieces made of metal and plastic.

Roy talked as he worked, describing what he was doing like he was talking to himself.

"Oh boy, this one's a doozy," he'd say. "Needs a whole new transmission." Then he would explain each thing he did, not caring if Noel paid attention or not. Without even trying, the teen absorbed knowledge like he was sawdust soaking up an oil spill.

Finally, after a month of doing grunt work, Noel got a chance to do something interesting.

Roy called him over. "Hey kid, want to give me a hand? I'm installing new brake pads."

Noel sauntered over like he wasn't excited at all. It was all the same to Roy but when they were done he offered a rare compliment.

"You're a natural, kid."

Each day, Noel learned a new skill. He could flush out a radiator, replace spark plugs, jumpstart or replace a battery. He could change oil, replace belts, rotate and align tires, fix a flat, replace a fuse and fix a slipping transmission.

Two months in, Noel asked "Where did you learn how to fix a car?"

Roy stopped what he was doing and looked Noel in the eye. "Prison."

Finally, it was Noel's last day working for Roy. He had a plan.

"Roy, man, if you need help on the weekends, I could come by, you wouldn't have to pay me or nothin'..."

Without a word, Roy handed him a box and waited for him to open it. It was a new mechanic tool kit and socket set.

"You earned it, Noel." It was the first time Roy hadn't called him kid. "Much as I'd love the help, your time with me is over. Take this card. My buddy owns a garage and I told him all about you. I said this kid ain't half-bad. He'll give you a job."

Noel shuffled his feet, speechless. Roy patted him on the shoulder. "You did good, kid."

The door opened just then and they turned to see Noel's probation officer walking in.

Roy nodded. "The kid passed with flying colors."

The probation officer said "I know, but that's not why I'm here. I think you know why, Roy."

Roy sighed. "Yep, been expecting you."

"You were doing so well, too. But dealing in stolen cars is a violation of your probation. I'm taking you in." He held up a pair of handcuffs.

Noel looked thunderstruck.

"It's okay, kid. Just promise me you'll choose door number one from now on."

"I promise, I swear!" He looked like he was about to cry.

"You go home now, it's been an honor working with you."

Hugging his socket set to his chest Noel ran out the door.

After pocketing the handcuffs that had been just

for show anyway, the probation officer walked over to the fridge and peered inside. "No beer?"

Roy laughed. "Not with the kid around. How many does that make?"

The officer popped open a soda. "I'd say a dozen or so. All those kids turning their lives around. Scared straight, huh?"

With a smile Roy took the remote from his pocket and music began to play. It was Elvis singing *Jailhouse Rock*. "Now, that's my favorite song."

FROM THE JAWS OF VICTORY

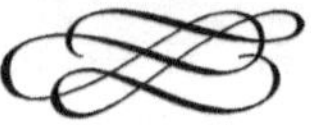

HER FATHER GUS HAD INSISTED ON NAMING HER Lorelei, a strong name for a strong woman he said. In German legend, Lorelei was a siren whose singing lured sailors to their doom on the cliffs of the Rhine. After learning its dark etymology her mother wasn't so keen on naming her precious girl after a serial killer but, in the end, she agreed as she planned to name their next child herself. Sadly, she had just the one.

Lorelei's earliest memory of her Uncle Charlie was her fifth birthday when he gave her an American Girl doll. She had politely handed it back explaining that dolls were boring. She preferred puzzles and math games. Even then, she felt free to speak her mind. Lorelei couldn't remember how old she was when she learned Charlie wasn't really her uncle; he was her father's business partner. The fact that her father was a genius she always knew. After all, his self-drilling rod for concrete forming was the company's only product.

When she was twelve, Lorelei's world came crashing down. After a terrible falling out, Charlie had booted her father from the company. Betrayed by his best friend, Gus began a downward spiral of depression and alcohol that ended, ironically, when his car hit a concrete wall made sturdy by his self-drilling rods. He had been hoisted with his own petard.

Grief altered the trajectory of Lorelei's life until she had only one goal: destroy Charlie. She attended college at sixteen with a double major in business and construction management and spent her free time studying trends in the construction industry, particularly sales of concrete. She excelled in everything she did but, to outsiders, she seemed obsessed. After graduation, she legally changed her last name to Rache, the German word for vengeance, in homage to her German father. She wasn't just being dramatic. She needed to infiltrate the company and although Charlie hadn't seen her since she was a child, and she had radically changed her appearance, her surname would've given away the game.

"I'm impressed with your in-depth knowledge of the industry, Ms. Rache," Charlie had said at the conclusion of her interview. "And your suggestions for improving efficiency are excellent. The job is yours if you want it. Your salary requirements--"

"—are flexible," Lori Rache replied with a smile. "It would be an honor to work for such an outstanding company. It's amazing what you've accomplished with just one patent."

A fleeting shadow crossed Charlie's face at the mention of her father's patent. It was the briefest instant, but Lori noted it.

"We're excited to have you on board," he said, "you can start Monday." He extended his hand to seal the deal. "I must say you look familiar, Ms. Rache, have we met before?"

She shook her head. "I don't think so. I've made presentations at several expos, maybe you saw me there."

He nodded. "That must be it."

It didn't take long for Lori Rache to become indispensable to the aging CEO. Over the next year, Charlie asked her advice about everything and she never steered him wrong. Yet, despite her stellar record, when she suggested they expand the factory he expressed concerns.

"We have no debt right now," he said, "and I'm uncomfortable taking out loans, especially at my age. I'm risk-averse," he joked.

"I understand," Lori said soothingly, "but the construction industry is booming and demand for our product is about to explode. We need to be ready."

She continued providing charts and graphs until he finally agreed to her plan.

She hadn't been lying about the coming construction boom but had omitted a key factor. The demand for their product was about to plummet. The federal government had recently contracted to build thousands of 3D-printed pre-fab houses to provide affordable housing. While the pre-fab process used lots of concrete, its molded forms didn't require self-drilling rods.

As Charlie's most trusted employee Lori was able to hide the truth from him about their falling sales. In the end, they were carrying too much debt from expanding a facility that was obsolete before it was built. The damage was done.

When Charlie called her into his office Lori had a powerful speech planned explaining what she'd done and why. Victory was so close it gave her goosebumps. Upon entering his office, however, she was taken aback by Charlie's haggard appearance and even felt a pang of sympathy for him. He invited her to take a seat.

"I want to tell you a story," he said, "about two friends who started a company together. One of the men was brilliant and creative, an inventor; the other was practical and organized. They built a thriving business but it turned out the inventor had a gambling problem. When he started stealing from the company, his partner looked the other way, hoping he would stop. Finally, when they couldn't meet payroll because the money had been gambled away, the partner told his friend to get help or get out. His friend refused and left the company. He drank himself to death within a year. The man never got over it, always wondering if he could've done more. He promised himself he would grow the business and, one day, he would gift it to his friend's only child, a smart little girl who thought dolls were boring."

He took Lori's hand. She was pale, in a state of shock. "I did it all for her. *For you*, Lorelei. And now it's gone. I'm so sorry."

Lorelei felt her blood run cold. She started sobbing, a release of years of pent-up anger and grief, and a mountain of regret.

"Oh, Uncle Charlie!"

She had no one to blame but herself. All that time planning his ruin when she was unwittingly planning her own. Charlie walked over and put his arm around her shoulders. He still loved her despite everything she'd done. A sense of calm eventually settled over her. She looked into his kind eyes with newfound resolve.

"I can fix this, Uncle Charlie. We can rise from the ashes."

He smiled and gave her shoulders a squeeze. "My money's on you, Lorelei. It always has been. Who do you think paid for your college?"

DUCK FOR COVER

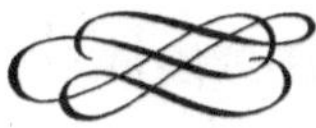

"I can't take it anymore," I was yelling into my phone. "These damn Muscovy ducks are everywhere, crapping on my driveway, nesting in my yard, trampling my flowers. What are you going to do about this nuisance, Harvey?"

The President of my homeowners' association sighed into the phone. "You know there's nothing I can do, Jerome. We've been over this many times."

"Okay," I said, "I'll pay for a removal service. I shouldn't have to spend my own money, but I will. I did it for the iguanas and I can do it for the ducks. Stupid invasive species," I muttered as I watched them through my kitchen window. Some of the males were bigger than my mother's cat. I couldn't afford to live on the lake and yet I was still plagued by these nasty birds. There was no justice in the world.

Harvey cleared his throat. "You can't do that without approval of the Board. Truth is, Jerome, a lot of people like the ducks."

"Truth is, Harvey, they're idiots. How do I bring this before the Board?"

"Make a motion through the website and ask for it to be on the next agenda."

"Fine. You've been as helpful as usual."

"Have a nice day, Jerome."

I opened the fridge and examined the sparse contents. Work had been so busy at the brokerage firm I hadn't had a chance to order groceries. No matter, I was dining out, my first date with the lovely Melissa. My new Tesla was waxed to perfection and charging up in the driveway. I had a reservation at Tiger Tiger, my favorite Asian fusion restaurant, sure to impress her. First dates were like a job interview, they can make or break you and I was taking no chances. After confirming Melissa was not a vegetarian I pre-ordered the chef's special for two, the most expensive dish on the menu. The chef required advance notice; this wasn't a dish you could order on a whim.

With some time to kill I decided to make a Cuban coffee the traditional way, on the stove top. As I waited for it to brew I saw my neighbor's kid through the window. She was feeding the ducks! I ran out the back door and vented all of my frustration on her.

"Get away from the ducks, Courtney! Did I say you could feed the ducks in my yard?"

Courtney started crying and her mother ran over to glare at me and shepherd her daughter into the house. I walked back in to find my smoke alarm blaring. The coffee had boiled over onto the burner causing billows of smoke. I turned off the stove and opened the back door to air out the house while I climbed on a chair to yank the battery out of the alarm. When I stepped down and turned around I faced my worst nightmare--a house full of ducks! Seeing the open door, they had invited themselves in. Muscovy ducks are silent so they can sneak up on you. I rushed them with my screwdriver in hand and they came for me. The biggest male chased me around the sofa trying to bite me. When they cornered me in the kitchen I was able to grab a broom and chase them back outside.

Heart racing, I sat down to catch my breath. I was effectively a prisoner in my own home, unable to open the back door without being assaulted by water fowl. The situation was intolerable. I marched over to my laptop and emailed the Board demanding they get rid of the ducks—or I would.

Feeling better, I shaved and dressed for my date but when I walked outside to unplug my Tesla from the charger I felt my blood pressure rise again. The ducks had crapped all over my clean car, the hood was a mess. They had even managed to sully the roof.

Cursing them every step of the way I uncoiled the garden hose and sprayed the car down. I couldn't wait to escape from the nine circles of hell I used to call home. As I tore out of the driveway I heard a piercing shriek that made my blood run cold. It was Courtney, standing on the sidewalk screaming her head off.

I opened my car window. "What's wrong, Courtney?"

With tears on her face she said "You almost ran over the baby ducks."

Gritting my teeth to keep profanities from flying out of my mouth I drove away. The farther I got from my house, the calmer I felt. With smooth jazz on the radio I could finally look forward to my date.

Melissa was right on time and seemed happy to see me. So far, so good. The host showed us to our table and I ordered the wine.

"Love this place," Melissa said. "I can't believe I've never been here before."

I smiled. "Wait until you taste the food, it's amazing."

We ordered appetizers and chatted like old friends as the wine loosened us up. Unfortunately, things went downhill when she asked me about my day. Somehow I couldn't stop myself from going on a rant about the ducks. I was on such a roll I didn't notice her reaction until it was too late.

"Do you know what I do for a living?" she asked

quietly.

I figured I was in trouble but didn't know why. "You're a professor at NSU, right?"

She shook her head. "You didn't even bother to Google me, did you? I'm a professor of ornithology."

I stared at her blankly.

"I study birds."

"Oh, I didn't know," I said.

"Clearly," she replied. "Can you guess what I wrote my thesis on?"

My heart sank. "Ducks?"

"Specifically, Muscovy ducks."

As I apologized for offending her and proclaimed myself a total dolt, the waiter brought the main course under a covered dome.

Melissa gave me a look. "You ordered dinner without asking me what I wanted?"

I didn't realize things could get worse but then they did. "I wanted to impress you by ordering the chef's specialty."

The waiter uncovered the chef's masterpiece: Peking Duck for two.

That was the end of my date. Melissa picked up her purse and left and I had our dinner packed to go.

I drove home wishing the day would just end already. I fell into bed and as I laid there in the dark I heard a rustling sound. I turned over and found myself peering into the beady little eyes of a very large duck. He looked mad.

MY CANADIAN GIRLFRIEND

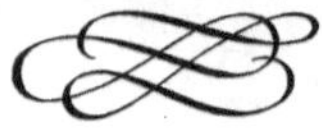

"Has he asked you for money yet?" her mother asked.

Chloe gritted her teeth. "Do you think I'm an idiot? Of course not."

Her mother continued loading plates into the dishwasher. "He could also be a bot. Have you seen typos or misspellings? Did you ask him to spell *potato* like I taught you?"

"Oh, my God! You're impossible." Chloe stood up and closed her laptop. She wanted to prep for her history test but her mother wouldn't stop pestering her. Studying at the kitchen table had been a bad idea. "Look, I know you're trying to help but I got this. I can handle my own love life."

Her mother froze, a statue of a woman holding a dirty dish in the air. "This isn't about your love life,

Chloe, it's about safety. If you get a service for free, then you're the product. Facebook uses everything it learns about you to attract advertisers, and don't get me started about WhatsApp. It has flaws that allow hackers to impersonate you--"

"--I know, Mom, you told me. Just because you're an IT expert doesn't mean I'm quitting social media. You want me to be a pariah? Look at my friends who used dating apps and got married: Ashley, Bob, Marguerite. It's not like it used to be when you were dating, it's hard to meet people. I thought you'd appreciate using computer science to find a soulmate."

Her mother sat down at the table with a sigh. "Of course I do, I helped develop a dating app, but that's not the point. This guy you're chatting with on What-sApp—*if he's even human*—could be catfishing, or a scammer. Or a human trafficker. There's no way of knowing."

Chloe smiled. "Oh yes, there is." She picked up her phone and within a minute was video-chatting with a handsome young man seated at a desk in his bedroom. "Hey Santiago! How's it going, babe? Will you please tell my mom you're real?" With that, Chloe shoved the phone in front of her mother.

"Hi, Mrs. H! I'm real. How's life in Toronto? It snowed today in New York City." He pointed the camera out the window so she could see the snow.

After exchanging pleasantries her mother handed

the phone to Chloe who promised her beau they would talk later.

"Happy now?" Chloe asked knowing full well her mother would never be satisfied.

Taking her daughter's hand she said "He seems like a nice boy but long-distance relationships rarely work out. I don't want you to get hurt. Your university has sixty thousand students and half of them are male, that's a big pool of candidates. Surely, there are some interesting guys in your classes."

Chloe laughed. "They're not *candidates*, mother. It's not a job interview. And I like Santiago a lot. He gets me."

"You don't know him, sweetheart. You don't know his friends, his family. You've only seen one side of him, the side he chooses to show you."

Chloe opened the fridge and poured herself a glass of milk. "You don't have to worry so much, okay? I'm a grown-up now." She kissed her mother on the cheek. "If it makes you feel any better, Santiago's mom says the same stuff to him. And she's a computer nerd, like you. Just think how smart our kids would be!"

"Are you sure?" her mother teased. "Being a computer nerd doesn't usually skip a generation."

"Very funny. Your comedy routine could use some work."

"I won't quit my day job." Her mother laughed. "Just think about what I said, okay?"

"Okay, fine."

~

As the weeks went by, Chloe's online relationship showed no signs of slowing down. When she casually mentioned that she planned to visit Santiago over Spring Break her mother's anxiety grew tentacles that snaked through her body. Part of her knew she was being irrational but she just couldn't let go of her fears. Terrible people lurked in the world of the internet. Nobody could be trusted and everyone had an angle.

One night, she couldn't sleep and did something she wasn't proud of. She hacked into her daughter's WhatsApp account and read the messages Chloe and Santiago had exchanged from the beginning. While she didn't see anything that troubled her, she still didn't want Chloe to go to New York to meet a total stranger. That was the basis for every episode of Unsolved Mysteries. Desperate times called for desperate measures. Using malware called FakesApp she pretended to be Chloe and sent Santiago a message saying she was having second thoughts about visiting. To her surprise, he replied immediately and said he was too. Then he wrote that he thought they should see other people. She was angry—nobody would treat her daughter like that! She messaged back that she didn't want him to contact her again and she could do so much better. He wrote back that he doubted it, but that was her loss. They continued trading barbs until they ran out of hurtful things to say. Chloe's mother was so distraught she didn't sleep at all.

In the morning, she stayed in bed until she was sure Chloe had left the house. She had made such a mess of things and she couldn't take it back. Her daughter would never forgive her. That night, Chloe didn't come home and her mother was worried. Chloe wouldn't answer her texts or calls, but who could blame her? The next afternoon Chloe finally called over Facetime. Her mother braced herself for the storm, but it didn't come. Chloe looked ecstatic.

"Where are you?" her mother asked.

"I'm in Cancun," Chloe said, sipping a frozen drink. "While you were busy breaking up with Santiago's mom over WhatsApp, we eloped." She turned the phone camera towards her new husband.

"Hi, Mrs. H!" Santiago said, beaming at her. "Is it okay if I call you Mom?"

I'LL DRINK TO THAT

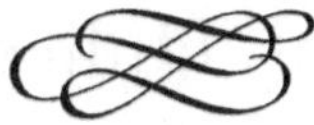

My head bartender Jama nods, deftly juggling three shot glasses to prove it. They're empty, of course. If she could make full glasses fly through the air she wouldn't need to work for me. Tonight was *The Battle of the Bartenders* between Casablanca, my bar, and The Gin Joint, which was directly across the street. Yes, we had lost *The Battle of the Bands* the month before, but we won the *Food Truck Extravaganza* in April when our own Mr. Cheezy beat Streetsa Pizza by three votes. It was a real squeaker. Cholesterol levels surely skyrocketed that day, a dream come true for Big Pharma. They should consider sponsoring Mr. Cheezy.

In case you're wondering how two Casablanca-themed bars wound up across from each other, it was no accident. More like a case of obsession, if not outright stalking. Imitation may be the highest form of flattery but it's also damn annoying, especially since I'm the Bogart fan, the guy who memorized every line of *Casablanca* and saved his money to open the bar he'd always dreamed of. Unlike Ricardo, who waited for me to open my bar before opening his across the street, the guy who stole my idea and has followed me around since we were kids. He even calls himself Rick now to pretend he's Bogart in *Casablanca*. If my parents had bought a house in a different subdivision, my life could've been so different. Coulda, woulda, shoulda, right?

It all started with the sixth-grade spelling bee. I'm not kidding. We were the last two standing and I took first place after Ricardo choked on the word syzygy and I spelled it correctly. A syzygy occurs when the sun, the Earth, and the moon line up for a lunar eclipse, also called a blood moon. It comes from the Greek word syzygos, which means yoked together. Somehow, that word sealed my fate and I've been yoked together with Ricardo ever since. Oh, irony, you playful minx, I could just strangle you.

After Ricardo opened The Gin Joint he appropriated every promotion idea I came up with. If I partnered with a charity, he did too. When I invented a signature drink and called it *We'll Always Have Paris*, he called his *Round Up the Usual Suspects*. When I sponsored a local sports team, he sponsored their rivals. When Casablanca set a Guinness World record for most eggs cracked in a minute with one hand, The Gin Joint set one for most aluminum cans crushed with an elbow in one minute. I finally gave up. I stopped trying to stay ahead and just coordinated with him. We were still competing constantly but we drew more patrons when we worked together. Local news stations loved us because we kept their ratings high. We celebrated the end of Prohibition every December 5th with a city-wide Pub Crawl. We had a funny costume contest for dogs in August for National Dog Day. Ricardo, aka Rick, kept me on my toes, I'll give him that. Honestly, I thought he would bankrupt me but we both did very well for ourselves. Then everything changed. Two weeks after *The Battle of the Bartenders*—which we won, thanks to Jama—The Gin Joint closed. There was no announcement, no explanation, just a sign on the door thanking the patrons for their friendship and the staff for their dedication. It also recommended that they try *Casablanca* across the street.

I was flabbergasted. I couldn't imagine why Ricardo would throw in the towel unless he had a devastating illness or...I couldn't think of any other reason. You'd think I would be relieved, happy to be rid of him after all this time, but I felt a little lost. More than a little. Who was Superman without Lex Luthor? Batman without the Joker? I was sure Ricardo thought of us as Batman and Robin, but I never did.

Six months later, I received a text with a picture of a gorgeous yacht at sea with two beautiful girls on deck drinking champagne with Ricardo. The name of the boat? *Here's Looking at You, Kid.*

I texted: "Wow! Don't tell me that's your yacht."

He replied: "You know it, Bro."

"But how?"

"I invested in crypto in 2009. I'm rich as hell. I could've quit anytime but I was having too much fun."

I tried to wrap my head around this news. I finally replied "Congrats! Where are you now?"

"I'm in Greece, I needed to arrive in time for the big event."

"What are you talking about?" I asked.

"I'm here for the lunar eclipse, of course. Maybe you're familiar with it? It's called a syzygy and it's spelled S-Y-Z-Y-G-Y."

WHATEVER THE WIDGET

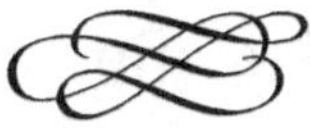

"I'd like to speak to Janice," the man said.

"This is Janice," Janice said patiently.

As anyone could attest, Janice never lost her cool. She was so upbeat and unflappable, so prepared and smart, her college friends called her Jandroid, a nickname she secretly loved. She was the Michelangelo of efficiency—it was her calling—and like Il Divino himself, once she chiseled away the superfluous, beauty would emerge. Chaos was the enemy and nobody understood that better than Janice. Wasted time, wasted movement, wasted inventory sent shivers up her spine. She knew in her heart everyone craved order and symmetry and that she could make it happen.

"Janice?" He sounded like he was lost at sea, clinging to a tattered raft that had sprung a leak.

"This is Hank Miller and I need your help. My business is going to hell in a handbasket. They say if it ain't broken, don't fix it, but I let it go on too long. Now I'm in trouble six ways to Sunday."

Janice found his colloquialisms charming and his neediness utterly endearing. A therapist would call her a rescuer and she would cheerfully agree.

"I can help, Hank," she reassured him. "What's the name of your business?"

"Put a cork in it."

"Excuse me?" To Janice, rudeness was never personal, just poor communication.

"That's the name of my business, *Put A Cork In It*. We sell cork stoppers and print logos on them."

"Fascinating," Janice said and she meant it. The world was a giant jigsaw puzzle and she enjoyed seeing how the pieces fit together. "What problems are you experiencing?"

Hank hesitated. "Hard to explain, better if I show you. When can you come?"

Janice's pulse quickened. Although she had been a superstar at her job straight out of college, Hank was the first client at *Whatever the Widget,* her fledgling enterprise. She relished the chance to establish herself and polish her reputation like a shiny apple.

"The total fee will depend on the situation," she explained, "but my hourly rate is—"

"—fine with me," Hank said. "You're my one chance to save the business."

High on adrenaline, Janice launched into her spiel. "As an efficiency expert, I help businesses become more profitable by improving organizational structure and development plans. An efficient operation uses analytics to reduce transaction time, eliminate bottlenecks, and optimize communication to decrease wait times, increase sales, and enhance the consumer and employee experience. I'll meet with key operators to observe the operation, understand the process, and collect relevant data. Rest assured, I analyze data at the most granular level and take a holistic approach to maximize operational efficiency. I then provide tactical solutions ranging from minor operational adjustments to facility or organizational changes."

She paused to take a breath, waiting for Hank to be dazzled. When he said nothing, she asked: "Do you have any questions?"

"Uh, well, I can't say I understood anything you just said. It kinda hurt my brain to try."

Janice didn't want to scare Hank off. "I'm sorry about that. To sum up, I'll determine what pain points in the process you can reduce or eliminate."

Hank laughed. "Pain, I understand. I'm in a world of it right now. I do have one question."

"Yes?"

"Can you come tomorrow?"

~

Janice spent the rest of the afternoon doing what she loved: research. Absorbing relevant facts would give her a head start and more credibility. She called it the wow factor. After reviewing the website for *Put A Cork In it* and taking copious notes on its shortcomings, she searched for clues to Hank's existential crisis but came up empty. She did learn that cork was harvested from cork oaks in Portugal and that corks were the preferred way to seal wine and liquor bottles (popularized by Dom Perignon in the early 16th century—who knew?) She watched videos on how corks were made and imprinted, impressed by all the information online. Cork was incredibly versatile: it was used in building materials, printers, clothing, cars, trains, rockets, skincare, glass-blowing, arts and crafts, sporting equipment and, of course, bulletin boards. There was even a market for used wine corks. Cork was so absorbent it had to be protected from smells of any kind. Janice could relate: nothing sent her running from a room like a noisome odor. Her nose was her Achilles heel but, on the plus side, she could smell a ripe mango from a block away.

The next morning, bedecked in business suit and heels, Janice waited for Hank at the entrance. *Put A Cork In It* was housed in a warehouse near the railroad tracks. Cheap rent reduced overhead, no room for improvement there. Janice made a note.

"You came!" Hank shook her hand with gusto. If

he was surprised at her youth it didn't show. Any port in a storm would do.

They toured the factory and he introduced her to his management team: Alberto in manufacturing, Luanne in quality control, and Mavis in shipping. None of them looked happy to see her but she didn't take offense. Janice was the harbinger of change and these three looked very set in their ways. Hank had been in business for twenty years manufacturing three grades of cork stoppers, all of which could be embossed with a logo for an extra fee. As Janice suspected, Alberto, Luanne, and Mavis had been with him since the start.

"Tell me about the problems you're having," Janice said when they were seated in his office.

Hank sighed. "You name it, everything's gone wrong. Manufacturing has slipped up, filling orders twice or not at all. Quality control sent out corks with crooked logos in the wrong colors. Something's gummed up in shipping too, orders keep getting returned with no explanation." He leaned in, brow furrowed. "I don't know why this is happening. My people were always reliable."

Janice looked up from her notes. "Are they angry with you? Passive-aggressive behavior at work is not uncommon."

Hank shrugged. "I've asked them straight out and they deny it. They got bonuses this year and a raise. Plenty of vacation too."

"Maybe it's time to clean house, start over?"

He shook his head. "I'm loyal to the core and don't toss people aside if I can help it."

Janice nodded sympathetically. "Any friction between them?"

Hank laughed. "Are you kidding? Those three are best friends. They bowl together every Wednesday night."

She stood up. "I'll need to interview them."

"Have at it," Hank said. "I hope you can figure this out."

Janice smiled. "I always do."

∽

The first thing she noticed in Mavis's office was the smell of flowers, specifically jasmine and gardenias. There were boxes of corks lined up against the front wall, labelled and sealed, ready to ship.

"I've been here so long I could do this job in my sleep," she joked nervously.

Janice nodded. "Tell me, Mavis, why do you think corks are being rejected so often? This seems to be a new development."

Mavis chewed on the end of her pencil, thinking. "It's a mystery. When I ask the customers, they say the wine tastes different but they can't explain it. We've run all kinds of tests in the lab. I'm sure we'll get to the bottom of it if we keep looking."

"I see." Janice made a note on her tablet. "That's all I have for now. By the way, what perfume are you wearing? It's nice."

Mavis blushed. "I love it too. It was a gift from Alberto. I mean, it's not what you're thinking, he was my Secret Santa."

"I wasn't thinking anything," Janice said disarmingly and waved on her way out.

Alberto stood when she walked into his office and invited her to take a seat. He offered her a donut from a box on his desk. Janice declined.

"What do you think is going on with manufacturing, Alberto? Why are there so many problems lately?"

He smiled confidently. "Those were minor glitches, they happen sometimes but I'm on top of it. I told Hank he can count on me."

Janice didn't comment but kept writing. She didn't even look up.

Alberto lost a bit of swagger when faced with silence. "Okay, I had a lapse of concentration, just some personal issues, but I'm good. It's all good."

She smiled. "I understand. Is there anything you'd like to tell me about Mavis? Or Luanne? I'm going to see her next."

His face lit up. "Oh, Luanne makes me laugh, she's so funny. Would you mind taking her a donut? It's her favorite kind."

"Sure, thanks for your time."

Janice had an inkling as to what was going on and her talk with Luanne confirmed it.

"I come bearing gifts," she said, placing the donut on Luanne's desk next to a framed photograph of Luanne and Mavis with a bowling trophy.

Luanne looked surprised, caught off-guard, but she was gracious. "That's my favorite, thank you."

"It's from Alberto," Janice said, watching her. A micro-expression flashed across Luanne's face but it wasn't pleasure, it was annoyance.

"Why do you think there are problems with the printing process, Luanne?"

She looked embarrassed, flustered. "I think it happened when I was training some new people. I wasn't supervising them as closely as I should have."

Janice took notes. "I see. Tell me about that picture on your desk."

Luanne relaxed her tense posture and picked up the picture. "That's the night we won the championship, Mavis bowled a perfect game. She's really something." Luanne's tone was warm, affectionate.

"That's all I need. Thank you, Luanne. Enjoy your donut."

Janice knocked lightly on Hank's open door. "I figured out your problem."

Hank looked up from his papers and invited her

in. "Already? You're the cat's pajamas, you are. Lay it on me, what kind of shape are we in?"

"I'm afraid the shape you're in is a triangle."

"Excuse me?" Hank scratched his head.

"You have a people problem. I can fix process, or systems, or chains of command, but I can't fix people."

Hank looked confused. "What do you mean? What triangle? What people?"

Janice laid her hands on the desk. "Mavis is in love with Alberto. Alberto is in love with Luanne. Luanne is in love with Mavis. None of them can focus. Also, Mavis's perfume is ruining the corks."

"What am I going to do?" Hank asked.

"You have a decision to make. Are you in business for love, or money?" She stood up, impervious to the shocked expression on Hank's face. "It's been a pleasure, Hank, I'll send you my invoice. Thank you for your business. If you could leave a review online, I'd appreciate it."

In the parking lot, Janice smiled to herself. Whatever the widget, she could always solve the problem. If her college friends had been there she knew what they'd say: Jandroid strikes again!

SEE YOU AT THE MOVIES

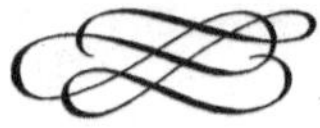

But Sean didn't know what to do. He reread his grandfather's final text as if this time it would make sense. Of course Grandpa Joe would use the last line of *Toy Story* 3 to say good-bye—movies were their thing—but *Citizen Kane* muttering about Rosebud would've been less cryptic.

He stared out the window of the plane in numb silence. Usually on the flight from New York to Fort Lauderdale Sean would watch a movie so he could discuss it with his grandfather. Then, after dinner, they'd sit on Grandpa Joe's patio with a cold beer and banter about plot holes, special effects, hokey dialogue, and which movies deserved an Oscar. His grandfather wasn't a fan of CGI—he claimed it wasn't acting—but after Sean showed him clips of

Andy Serkis as Gollum crawling around in a motion capture suit, he was on board. His mother joked that, for movie buffs, they weren't very discriminating, and it was true. They would watch almost anything, sometimes just for the pleasure of tearing it apart. Of the fifty worst movies on Rotten Tomatoes they'd probably seen half of them, including bombs like *Jaws: The Revenge* and *Highlander II: The Quickening*. After a critic described *Highlander II* as "almost awesome in its badness", that became their catchphrase. If Sean said a movie stunk, Grandpa Joe would say: "Yes, but was it awesome in its badness?" and they'd crack up.

Whenever they watched a movie together they made popcorn, their version of a tailgate party. They would quiz each other on obscure movie facts like it was their secret language. On the day Grandpa Joe revealed his diagnosis to Sean, he said: "I'm not afraid to die. Although it wouldn't be my first choice." With tears in his eyes Sean said "Seriously? *Bridge of Spies?*" and his grandfather smiled. After patting Sean affectionately on the back he said he wanted to watch *The Bucket List*, and not because he was being morbid. He was just hoping for a laugh and a fresh perspective. Sean realized then how much solace his grandfather found in movies. As Sean microwaved the popcorn he said: "Fine, but if you make me watch *Death at a Funeral*, I'm outta here, old man."

Once the credits rolled, Grandpa Joe became

philosophical. "Movies show you how to live your life. It's about one person's quest to learn that what they want isn't always what they need."

Sean grabbed a handful of popcorn. "How about *The Terminator*, did he learn anything?"

"It may have been called *The Terminator* but it was Sarah Connor's story."

"True. How about *Game of Thrones?* There were dozens of characters, whose story was that?"

Grandpa Joe smiled. "Jon Snow's, of course. The finale was a fiasco because the writers forgot who the protagonist was."

Sean was suddenly pulled out of his reverie by a flight attendant with a beverage cart. On a whim, he purchased a beer and turned towards the window to toast his grandfather. He remembered a line from *The Second Best Marigold Hotel*: "There is no such thing as an ending, just a place where you leave the story." He imagined Grandpa Joe responding with a quote from *Gladiator*: "Death smiles at us all. All a man can do is smile back."

Then it came to him. Sean knew what he needed to do. After powering up his laptop he got to work. As soon as the plane touched down he called a party equipment rental service and also the funeral home to set his plan in action. His mother was grateful he wanted to take charge.

Everything was in place on the day of the memorial service. When Sean took the podium and faced the crowd, a big-screen TV loomed behind him.

"As you all know, my grandfather was my best friend. He taught me so much about life through his love of movies. If he were here now he would say: a funeral is an amazing tradition. They throw a great party for you on the one day they know you can't come. That's from *The Big Chill*. One of his favorite quotes, though, was from *Ferris Bueller's Day Off*: "Life moves pretty fast. If you don't stop and look around once in a while, you could miss it." Now, ain't that the truth? To be honest, I wasn't sure how to honor Grandpa Joe's memory, but then it came to me. I turned his life into a movie with a score of his favorite soundtracks." Sean signaled and a theater-sized popcorn machine was wheeled in, replete with fresh, warm popcorn that smelled delicious.

"Please grab a bag of popcorn and enjoy the show. And Grandpa Joe, I leave you with a quote from *John Q*: "No goodbye, you know I don't like goodbyes. See you later!""

BRAVE NEW WORLD

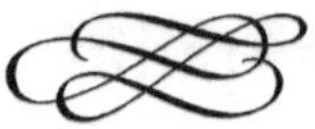

"How would you like to pay for that?" the shopkeeper asked brightly. "Credit card? Debit?"

The elderly woman shook her head stubbornly. "Neither."

"I accept Venmo, Zelle, Google Pay, Apple Pay and PayPal. Also Crypto, depending on which one."

The woman fumbled in her coat pocket and pulled out four twenties. "I don't even know what those words mean, young lady, but I do have cash."

The shopkeeper sighed and cast a rueful eye towards the counter. Items that should have been deducted from inventory were still hers to keep—and reshelve. Her sympathies extended to the true victim here--her. She pointed to the sign on the wall: *Cash not accepted.*

Undaunted, the erstwhile customer, whose name was Nora, laid a twenty on the counter. "Let me show you something. See the words across the top of this bill? *Federal Reserve Note.* Now, look toward the bottom, to the left of that slave trader Andrew Jackson, you see what it says? *This note is legal tender for all debts public and private.* That means I can use it to pay for stuff, here, there, everywhere. It's the coin of the realm."

"Not here, it isn't."

Reaching into her other pocket Nora produced a variety of coins and bills. "Fine, then I can pay with euros, rupees, yen, or pounds. Your choice."

The shopkeeper sniffed dismissively. "I don't even know what those words mean, ma'am. But no cash means no cash. Good day."

With a huff Nora grabbed a handful of free samples of crackers on her way out the door. As she walked she munched on gluten-free sesame rice crackers and wondered how she found herself in this position. Nothing made sense anymore. All her friends were dead, senile, or in retirement homes playing bingo and eating overcooked food. That was God's waiting room and she, for one, wasn't having it. She could wait for God in the comfort of her own home, thank you very much. On top of that, nobody talked to each other anymore. They were always staring at their phones, even when crossing the street.

It was a wonder they weren't all roadkill, run over by drivers also mesmerized by their phones. In restaurants, at playgrounds, while walking their dogs, people only cared about their phones. They missed everything! Nora may have been a Luddite, but at least she enjoyed a beautiful day where butterflies flitted by.

Spotting a small café ahead Nora went in. She didn't see any signs posted that cash wasn't accepted so she took a chance. The baked goods display made her mouth water; a buttery croissant and coffee would hit the spot. After seating herself at a table in the corner she waited to be served. No one brought her a menu so she stopped a busboy passing by.

"I'd like to order, please."

"Sure," he said without stopping. "Just use the QR code on your table."

Nora turned to a man sitting behind her. "What's a QR code?"

He looked up from his phone. "There's a black and white square on your table. Point your phone camera at it and it will bring up the menu. Then you order on the website and pay through your phone."

Nora shook her head at the world she lived in. "Thanks, I guess I'm not that hungry." And she left.

After walking a few blocks she saw a patch of green where a woman in a straw hat was working away.

"Good morning!" straw-hat lady said with a wave.

Nora smiled. "It is a good morning, isn't it? What are you doing?"

"Gardening. This is our community center, would you like a tour?"

"I'd love one," Nora said and then hesitated. "Is there a charge?"

The woman laughed and it sounded like wind chimes. "It's free and I'll even give you a gift at the end."

Nora spent the next hour with her new friend Sage admiring the three dozen garden plots, trying to guess what was growing in each. There were vegetable varieties she didn't know and purple cauliflowers she found delightful. She helped Sage do some weeding and marveled at how time passed so quickly. Handing her a bag filled with vegetables Sage invited her to come back anytime and to join their weekly potluck supper the next day.

Soon, Nora became a regular at the community center and her eggplant parmesan was a crowd favorite at the potlucks. She spent all her time gardening with her new friends. She even bought a straw hat. One day, Sage asked if she would mind working the register at their small farmers' market. Of course Nora said she would do it. During her first shift, a woman presented her basket to be rung up and Nora had to stifle a laugh. It was her nemesis, the haughty shopkeeper.

"That will be forty dollars and seventy-five cents," she said.

When the shopkeeper tendered her credit card, Nora shook her head and pointed gleefully at the sign on the wall: *Cash only*.

THAT DARING YOUNG MAN

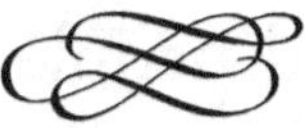

"Dude, you joined a circus? Why would you do that?" Max ordered another round of drinks.

Brett polished off his lager and started on the fries. "Because my girlfriend said I was boring. Right before she broke up with me."

"Harsh," Max sympathized. "But I still don't get it. Were you trying to win her back?" He looked thoughtful. "Did you have some kind of breakdown? I mean, you're a marketing major, not a lion tamer."

Brett laughed. "It's not that kind of circus. Think Cirque du Soleil but with kids. I applied for a marketing position. When I didn't get it, they offered me tent crew. I figured why not?"

Max leaned back in his bar stool. "I can think of some reasons. Sounds like a punishment to me."

"Oh, it was," Brett said. "I knew it was a mistake

the minute I got there. The first day, we were setting up the big top and I almost got crushed by the main pole. It was just a summer job but I've never worked so hard in my life. Not only did we stake these huge tents, we also had to assemble heavy aluminum seating for six hundred people. Then, two days later, we'd break it down in the dead of night—sometimes in the pouring rain—load it on trucks, and drive to the next town to do it all over again. There were a million ways to get hurt but my biggest fear was getting bear claw."

"I'm guessing you don't mean the pastry," Max said wryly.

Brett shook his head. "Ha, I wish! No, it's when your hand gets permanently stuck in a claw position from nerve damage."

"Brutal," Max said. "Put that in your dating profile, I dare you. *Rugged outdoors type, my spirit guide is a bear.*"

"Funny." Brett finished the fries and pushed the basket away. "Don't get me started about the living conditions. I slept in an RV with five other guys, no hot showers, barely any Wi-Fi. I read some long, boring books, let me tell you. And one of my roommates was a guy named Smiley, total weirdo. The icing on the cake."

"How was the food?"

"Pretty good, actually. I never had quinoa for breakfast before, but I liked it."

"I hate to ask the obvious," Max said, "but why didn't you just quit?"

"I thought about it every day," Brett admitted, "but I'm not a quitter and I didn't want to leave them shorthanded."

"Well," Max said, "what doesn't kill us makes us stronger, right?"

Brett smiled. "It wasn't all bad."

"You dog! Did you find a girl? Who was she, like a bearded lady?"

Brett choked on his beer and they both cracked up. "No girls, no guys either. Just something amazing."

"Go on."

"One day, I wandered into the big top and one of the instructors was prepping for her next class. She asked if I wanted a trapeze lesson. I said yes before I could think about it. She taught me how to stand, how to swing my legs up, how to fall. Then she put the safety belt around my waist and told me to chalk up my hands in the chalk bucket. I climbed up the ladder and looked down from the perch."

"You're deathly afraid of heights, buddy," Max interjected.

"You're telling me," Brett said. "But I watched her do it first and there was a safety net."

"How did you do? Don't leave me hanging."

"I was terrified and exhilarated at the same time. I thought for sure I would throw up. Jumping off that tiny platform was suddenly the biggest decision of my life. Of course, I was holding onto the trapeze swing when I jumped and I managed to throw my legs over and hang upside down. Then I fell into the net. It was like flying and thinking you're going to die at the same time. I screamed all the way down but everyone does that their first time."

"Wow! Did you do it again?"

Brett grinned. "Lots of times."

"I'm jealous, man. That's life-changing stuff."

"Yeah, it was. Sometimes I dream I'm on the trapeze," Brett said wistfully. "Honestly, that was the best summer of my life."

EVERY AGE ALL AT ONCE

"I READ SOMEWHERE THAT EVERY AGE WE'VE EVER been is stored in our brain like an onion, layer upon layer. Weird, right?" Two glasses of wine always made Clara philosophical.

"I can't hear you," Melanie said. "The two-year-old in my brain is throwing a tantrum."

Clara laughed. "Give her a cookie, she'll calm down." They raised their glasses, pretended to clink them through the computer screen. They loved their weekly video chats.

"Have you thought about our anniversary?" Melanie asked. "Fifty years is a milestone." She scooped up her grandson Robin, playing on the floor by her feet. No stranger to Zoom calls Robin was excited to show Clara his new toy.

"Great truck, buddy!" Clara said. "You mean, our

Friendaversary?" She sipped her wine as she considered it. "Let's see, if we were fourteen, we could celebrate by hanging out at the mall, trying on everything and buying nothing. Those Orange Juliuses were nasty, right? Our high school selves would go to the football game and then Figaro's for pizza. How old were we in Girl Scouts? Remember camping in those leaky tents when it stormed like crazy? Good times."

"I knew there was a reason I hated camping," Melanie said. "I must have blocked that one out. I liked our long bike rides in the summer when we got hot and sweaty and rode to 7-11 for a Slurpee."

"That was the best, brain freeze notwithstanding."

"Totally worth it," Melanie agreed.

"What's brain freeze?" Robin asked.

"It's an ouchie that goes away fast," Melanie explained.

Losing interest, Robin went to chase the dog and bumped into a table. He wailed for Grandma.

"Laughing leads to crying," Melanie said. "Gotta run. Let's think about it and make a plan—something wild and crazy and totally out of character."

"Sure, that sounds like us." Clara blew her a virtual kiss and signed off.

Clara was determined to make their anniversary special. She had too many regrets, remembered too many lost opportunities, imbuing her with a new sense of urgency. Six decades on earth will do that to a person. One of her regrets was not recognizing special moments; it was like receiving a basket of beautiful fruit and forgetting to eat them. She knew she was too low key, a cautionary tale for others: This is your life, pay attention. Afraid she wasn't up to the task of planning something grand, she Googled possible adventures: cruises, spa weekends, antiquing, llama ranches, cooking lessons with world-class chefs, wine tours. In an effort to be wild and crazy and totally out of character, she perused white water rafting, skydiving, bungee jumping, scuba lessons, and wilderness survival, knowing they would never find the nerve to do any of them. There was just as much chance of them learning the art of Ninja in Japan or building their own igloo in Greenland. Nothing seemed right. Clara thought she hit the jackpot when she discovered treehouse vacations with all the amenities. That looked like fun! She was about to share the links with Melanie when she caught the news: a raging pandemic just put the kibosh on any Friendaversary event.

The next two years transpired outside of normal time. Days were impossibly long but months were gone in the blink of an eye. Melanie had to help out with her grandchildren; Clara's son had medical issues. When life calmed down a bit, although still not normal by any means, they talked about their overdue Friendaversary.

Melanie texted her: *Expect a special delivery on Friday. It's a surprise.*

No matter how she wheedled Clara couldn't pry out of her friend what she was up to. Friday morning, there was a loud revving sound outside Clara's door. She stepped outside to see a slim person in a leather jacket and jeans sitting on a Harley. The person waved and Clara waved back. Then the person took off their helmet.

"What are you doing?" Clara squealed, clapping her hands together and dancing around.

"Want to go for a ride?" Melanie smiled and handed her a helmet of her own.

"I don't know." Clara said, donning the helmet. "Does it come with a Slurpee?"

"You bet it does."

Then Clara hopped on and they rode off together to be wild and crazy and totally out of character. If you didn't count the Slurpee.

ABOUT THE AUTHOR

Award-winning author Barbara Venkataraman is an attorney in South Florida where she draws inspiration for her books from the daily headlines. She loves connecting with readers through her books and finds a particular kind of joy in a well-turned phrase. In addition to writing fiction, she co-authored *Accidental Activist: Justice for the Groveland Four* with her son Josh Venkataraman about his successful four-year quest to obtain posthumous pardons for The Groveland Four.

~

To learn more about Barbara Venkataraman and discover more Next Chapter authors, visit our website at www.nextchapter.pub.

Duck For Cover & Other Tales
ISBN: 978-4-82414-846-9
Large Print

Published by
Next Chapter
2-5-6 SANNO
SANNO BRIDGE
143-0023 Ota-Ku, Tokyo
+818035793528

26th October 2022

www.ingramcontent.com/pod-product-compliance
Lightning Source LLC
LaVergne TN
LVHW091526170726
843492LV00004B/1086